HAPPY POEMS chosen by Roger McGough

MACMILLAN CHILDREN'S BOOKS

With thanks to my editor Gaby Morgan
who continues to champion poetry for children,
and my researcher Hilary McGough

First published 2018 by Macmillan Children's Books
an imprint of Pan Macmillan
20 New Wharf Road, London N1 9RR
Associated companies throughout the world
www.panmacmillan.com

ISBN 978-1-5098-7137-7

1 3 5 7 9 8 6 4 2

A CIP catalogue record for this book is available from
the British Library.

Printed and bound by CPI Group (UK) Ltd, Croydon CR0 4YY

Contents

A Smile

Smiling is infectious,
you catch it like the flu.
When someone smiled at me today
I started smiling too.

I passed around the corner
and someone saw my grin.
When he smiled, I realized
I'd passed it on to him.

I thought about my smile and then
I realized its worth.
A single smile like mine could travel
right around the earth.

If you feel a smile begin
don't leave it undetected.
Let's start an epidemic quick
and get the world infected.

Jez Alborough

Yes

A smile says: Yes.
A heart says: Blood.
When the rain says: Drink
The earth says: Mud.

The kangaroo says: Trampoline.
Giraffes say: Tree.
A bus says: Us,
While a car says: Me.

Lemon trees say: Lemons.
A jug says: Lemonade.
The villain says: You're wonderful.
The hero: I'm afraid.

The forest says: Hide and Seek.
The grass says: Green and Grow.
The railway says: Maybe.
The prison says: No.

The millionaire says: Take.
The beggar says: Give.
The soldier cries: Mother!
The baby sings: Live.

The river says: Come with me.
The moon says: Bless.
The stars say: Enjoy the Light.
The sun says: Yes.

Adrian Mitchell

The Laughter Forecast

Today will be humorous
With some giggly patches,
Scattered outbreaks of chuckling in the south
And smiles spreading from the east later,
Widespread chortling
Increasing to gale-force guffaws towards evening.
The outlook for tomorrow
Is hysterical.

Sue Cowling

from *Pippa Passes*

The year's at the spring
And day's at the morn;
Morning's at seven;
The hillside's dew-pearled;
The lark's on the wing;
The snail's on the thorn:
God's in His heaven –
All's right with the world!

Robert Browning

The Feeling of Having a Good Day

Hallelujah —
I'm awake!
This day belongs to me

and I'm its favourite.
It wants to lick me
like a dog.

The world
is a balloon
that's on my string.

I'll get a prize
at school assembly
for being me,

then all the lessons
will be about
my awesomeness

and at break
I'll kick the football
to Australia.

I can see it in the mirror
when I smile –
I have electric teeth!

Joanne Limburg

To See a World

To see a world in a grain of sand
And a heaven in a wild flower,
Hold Infinity in the palm of your hand
And Eternity in an hour.

William Blake

Hope on a Rope

If you don't
want to lose hope,
tie it to a rope and pull
yourself to safety. Because
hope has the power to lift
you up – whether your
troubles are
light or
w
e
i
g
h
t
y
.

Brian Bilston

The Teacher's Gift
(Margarette Nicholson, 1909–85)

Every time I tell the time
Or work out ten times two,
I open up a precious gift
Bequeathed to me by you.

You gave me names and numbers.
You taught me how to spell.
You told me how to hold a pen
And how to write as well.

You showed me how to read aloud
From books of red and blue.
You filled my head with goats and trolls
And tinderboxes too.

You planted seeds inside me
But did not see them grow.
A bell rings at the end of school
We pack our bags and go.

These words I scrawl on paper,
This shape upon my tongue,
Is made from things you gave to me
Way back when I was young.

Steve Turner

High Achievers

We thought we could . . .
We said we would
go on the climb
to Mount Sublime
and we did it! Yes! We did it!
We got to the top! We did it!

They said it was impossible.
They said we wouldn't last.
They said it was a grown-ups' walk
and grown-ups walk too fast.
They said you must be big and strong –
The path is very steep
and you have to cross some channels where
the water's very deep.
They said the climb is difficult
and we're not old enough
to know you just keep going when
the going's really tough.
They said there could be leeches and
creepy crawly things
and real explorers don't complain

of scratches, bites and stings.
They thought we wouldn't make it but
they let us go along
and we showed them, yes we showed them they
were wrong! wrong! wrong!

Kate O'Neil

Picking Teams

When we pick teams in the playground,
Whatever the game might be,
There's always somebody left till last
And usually it's me.

I stand there looking hopeful
And tapping myself on the chest,
But the captains pick the others first,
Starting, of course, with the best.

Maybe if teams were sometimes picked
Starting with the worst,
Once in his life a boy like me
Could end up being first!

Allan Ahlberg

Best Friends

It's Susan I talk to not Tracey,
Before that I sat next to Jane;
I used to be best friends with Lynda
But these days I think she's a pain.

Natasha's all right in small doses,
I meet Mandy sometimes in town;
I'm jealous of Annabel's pony
And I don't like Nicola's frown.

I used to go skating with Catherine,
Before that I went there with Ruth;
And Kate's so much better at trampoline:
She's a showoff, to tell you the truth.

I think that I'm going off Susan,
She borrowed my comb yesterday;
I *think* I might sit next to Tracey,
She's my nearly best friend: she's OK.

Adrian Henri

Oath of Friendship

Shang ya!
I want to be your friend
For ever and ever without break or decay.
When the hills are all flat
And the rivers are all dry,
When it lightens and thunders in winter,
When it rains and snows in summer,
When Heaven and Earth mingle –
Not till then will I part from you.

Anon. (China)

May You Always

May your smile be ever present
May your skies be always blue
May your path be ever upward
May your heart be ever true

May your dreams be full to bursting
May your steps be always sure
May the fire in your soul
Blaze on for evermore

May you live to meet ambition
May you strive to pass each test
May you find the love your life deserves
May you always have the best

May your happiness be plentiful
May your regrets be few
May you always be my best friend
May you always . . . just be you

Paul Cookson

Squeezes

We love to squeeze bananas,
We love to squeeze ripe plums,
And when they are feeling sad
We love to squeeze our mums.

Brian Patten

Don't

Don't comb your hair in company.
Don't cross the kitchen floor in welly boots.
Don't put the television on.
Don't squint. Don't get in fights.

Don't stuff your mouth with sausage.
Don't drop towels on the bathroom floor.
Don't hang about with that rough crowd.
Don't put your feet up on the chair.

Don't use up all the paper in the loo.
Don't scratch. Don't twitch. Don't sniff. Don't talk.
Don't stick your tongue out.
Don't you dare to answer back.

Life is full of opportunity, says my mum.

Barrie Wade

Mother to Son

Well, son, I'll tell you:
Life for me ain't been no crystal stair.
It's had tacks in it,
And splinters,
And boards torn up,
And places with no carpet on the floor –
Bare.
But all the time
I'se been a-climbin' on,
And reachin' landin's,
And turnin' corners,
And sometimes goin' in the dark
Where there ain't been no light.
So, boy, don't you turn back.
Don't you set down on the steps
'Cause you finds it kinder hard.
Don't you fall now –
For I'se still goin', honey,
I'se still climbin',
And life for me ain't been no crystal stair.

Langston Hughes

Two People

She reads the paper,
while he turns on TV;
she likes the mountains,
he craves the sea.

He'd rather drive,
she'll take the plane;
he waits for sunshine;
she walks in the rain.

He gulps down cold drinks,
she sips at hot;
he asks, 'Why go?'
She asks, 'Why not?'

In just about everything
they disagree,
but they love one another
and they both love me.

Eve Merriam

You Have a Body

You have a body.
You're not air.
You're not just anywhere,
you're THERE.
I suppose you might feel new with it,
wondering what you might do with it.

Those arms and legs
can be flung about.
You can walk
   or run
      or fall over
         FLAT
   which is, of course,
the problem with that.
You can breathe, you can gasp,
you can cough, sneeze or rasp.
You have fingers!
You can grasp!

And it's all yours
to do what you want with,
to turn right round or
face the front with.

Or mostly yours,
though some of it belongs
to your mum and dad
to remind them of the bodies
they once had.

And yet it's yours —
you'll see it grow
though not so that
you ever know.
It's fun, it's great,
something you learn to operate.
Just pinch yourself and see.
Who is that? It's YOU not me.

It's yours to wear and yours to be.
And it comes free!

George Szirtes

Three Good Things

At day's end I remember
three good things.

Apples maybe – their skinshine smell
and soft froth of juice.

Water maybe – the pond in the park
dark and full of secret fish.

A mountain maybe – that I saw in a film,
or climbed last holiday,
and suddenly today it thundered up
into a playground game.
Or else an owl – I heard an owl today,
and I made bread.
My head is full of all these things,
it's hard to choose just three.

I let remembering fill me up
with all good things
so that good things will overflow
into my sleeping self,

and in the morning
good things will be waiting
when I wake.

Jan Dean

The Cupboard

I know a little cupboard,
With a teeny tiny key,
And there's a jar of Lollipops
    For me, me, me.

It has a little shelf, my dear,
As dark as dark can be,
And there's a dish of Banbury Cakes
    For me, me, me.

I have a small fat grandmamma,
With a very slippery knee,
And she's Keeper of the Cupboard,
    With the key, key, key

And when I'm very good, my dear,
As good as good can be,
There's Banbury Cakes, and Lollipops
    For me, me, me.

Walter de la Mare

BOY GIRL

Boy	Girl
Garden	Gate
Standing	Kissing
Very	Late
Dad	Comes
Big	Boots
Boy	Runs
Girl	Scoots

Anon.

Isn't My Name Magical?

Nobody can see my name on me.
My name is inside
and all over me, unseen
like other people also keep it.
        Isn't my name magic?

My name is mine only.
It tells I am individual,
the only special person it shakes
when I'm wanted.

If I'm with hundreds of people
and my name gets called,
my sound switches me on to answer
like it was my human electricity.
        Isn't that magical?

My name echoes across playground,
it comes, it demands my attention.

I have to find out who calls,
who wants me for what.
My name gets blurted out in class,
it is a terror, at a bad time,
because somebody is cross.

My name gets called in a whisper
I am happy, because
my name may have touched me
with a loving voice.
  Isn't it all magic?

James Berry

Keeping Wicket

When they were young,
She kept wicket for her brothers,
They batted,
Bowled,
Padded up
And ratcheted up the score.
She crouched behind the stumps
Keeping wicket.

She would have loved to bowl,
Just once to flick her wrist and watch the ball
Fly from her fingers, arcing through the air,
To hear the thwack of
Rubber on bamboo.
To not worry that the batsman might miss,
Or worse still get an edge.

She would have liked to bat,
To feel the jerk of willow in her hands
And watch the leather careering
Towards the boundary,
But she was too valuable a player,
To be put in to bat.

She had the best job, they said.
The wicket-keeper held the destiny of the team
In those thin gloves.
The wicket-keeper was the team's protector.
A V.I.P.

So she crouched behind the stumps
Keeping wicket.
And when their mother developed
Into childhood,
Their diabetic father became an amputee,
They gave her the best job once again.
Her brothers were all busy at the crease,
So she crouched behind the stumps,
Keeping wicket.

She contemplated trying another game,
Was attracted to another life,
But though cricket is a man's game,
No man it seems wants a wicket-keeper for a wife.

And when her parents passed,
She still played the game,
This time with nieces and nephews at the crease,
She had the best job once again,
Standing behind the stumps,
Keeping wicket.

Valerie Bloom

My Sister

My sister's remarkably light,
She can float to a fabulous height.
It's a troublesome thing,
But we tie her with string,
And we use her instead of a kite.

Margaret Mahy

Middle Child

The piggy in the middle
The land between sky and sea
The cheese which fills the sandwich
The odd one out of three
The one who gets the hand-me-downs
And broken bits of junk
The follower, not the leader
The one in the bottom bunk

The one for whom the pressure's off
The one who can run wild
The one who holds the balance of power
The lucky second child.

Lindsay MacRae

Siblings

Like the Three Musketeers
we were all for one.

Like the Three Blind Mice
we saw without looking.

Like the Three Bowls of Porridge
we were just right.

Like the Three Sisters
we were sad inside.

Like the Three Billy Goats Gruff
we feared the troll.

Like the Three Little Pigs
we longed for our own home.

Like the Three Wishes
we were never enough.

                              Joseph Coelho

A Blessing

Just off the highway to Rochester, Minnesota,
Twilight bounds softly forth on the grass.
And the eyes of those two Indian ponies
Darken with kindness.
They have come gladly out of the willows
To welcome my friend and me.
We step over the barbed wire into the pasture
Where they have been grazing all day, alone.
They ripple tensely, they can hardly contain their
    happiness
That we have come.
They bow shyly as wet swans. They love each
    other.
There is no loneliness like theirs.
At home once more,
They begin munching the young tufts of spring in
    the darkness.
I would like to hold the slenderer one in my arms,
For she has walked over to me
And nuzzled my left hand.

She is black and white,
Her mane falls wild on her forehead,
And the light breeze moves me to caress her long ear
That is delicate as the skin over a girl's wrist.
Suddenly I realize
That if I stepped out of my body I would break
Into blossom.

James Wright

Paintings that Move

Across the sand or through the gorse,
leaping over Aintree's course
rides the wonder
called the Horse.

Royal duty, on parade,
gazing in a Sussex glade,
Gymkhana day
with tail of braid.

Plumed and brushed with chestnut sheen,
carries all from waif to queen,
and everyone
that's in between.

Galloping with Mustang fire.
Steaming still in Highland byre.
Filly, stallion,
Shetland, Shire.

Hear its heart and kiss its chin,
stroke the mane
and smell the skin,
neighing poems from within.

Athlete, best friend, loping grace.
Pegasus that knows its place.
Servant of
the human race.

Stewart Henderson

Heroes

Heroes are funny people, dey are lost an found
Sum heroes are brainy an sum are muscle-bound
Plenty heroes die poor an are heroes after dying
Sum heroes mek yu smile when yu feel like crying
Sum heroes are made heroes as a political trick
Sum heroes are sensible an sum are very thick!
Sum heroes are not heroes cause dey do not play
   de game
A hero can be young or old and have a silly name.
Drunks an sober types alike hav heroes of dere
   kind
Most heroes are heroes out of sight an out of mind,
Sum heroes shine a light upon a place where
   darkness fell
Yu could be a hero soon, yes, yu can never tell.
So if yu see a hero, better treat dem wid respect
Poets an painters say heroes are a prime subject,
Most people hav heroes even though some don't
   admit
I say we're all heroes if we do our little bit.

Benjamin Zephaniah

Cats

Cats sleep
Anywhere,
Any table,
Any chair,
Top of piano,
Window-ledge,
In the middle,
On the edge,
Open drawer,
Empty shoe,
Anybody's
Lap will do,
Fitted in a
Cardboard box,
In the cupboard
With your frocks –
Anywhere!
They don't care!
Cats sleep
Anywhere.

Eleanor Farjeon

Cat

My cat has got no name,
We simply call him Cat;
He doesn't seem to blame
Anyone for that.

For he is not like us
Who often, I'm afraid,
Kick up quite a fuss
If *our* names are mislaid.

As if, without a name,
We'd be no longer there
But like a tiny flame
Vanish in bright air.

My pet, he doesn't care
About such things as that:
Black buzz and golden stare
Require no name but Cat.

Vernon Scannell

Charlotte's Dog

Daniel the spaniel has ears like rugs,
Teeth like prongs of electric plugs.

His back's a thundery winter sky,
Black clouds, white clouds rumbling by.

His nose is the rubber of an old squash ball
Bounced in the rain. His tail you'd call

A chopped-off rope with a motor inside
That keeps it walloping. Red-rimmed-eyed,

He whimpers like plimsolls on a wooden floor.
When he yawns he closes a crimson door.

When he barks it's a shark of a sound that bites
Through frosty mornings and icy nights.

When he sleeps he wheezes on a dozing lung:
Then he wakes you too with a wash of his tongue!

Kit Wright

Tell It to the Dog

If you have had
an awful day
and no one wants
to come and play
and all your woes
won't go away,
just tell it to the dog.

If everybody
picks on you
and all your plans
have fallen through;
if you feel lonely,
sad and blue,
just tell it to the dog.

Dogs do not judge.
They understand.
They rub your leg.
They lick your hand.
If you feel lost
in no-man's-land
just tell it to the dog.

Dogs keep your secrets
safe within.
They don't care if
you lose or win.
So turn that frown
into a grin
and tell it to the dog!

(Or, failing that,
make do with the cat . . .)

Joshua Seigal

A Meerkat Lullaby

Hush pretty meerkitten don't you cry
Mummy will sing you a lullaby
Daddy on guard, is standing near
Ready to bark should danger appear

His back is straight, his hindlegs long
His hearing acute, his eyesight strong
So go to sleep my little beauty
Safe with Daddy on sentry duty.

Roger McGough

Weird Wildlife

It's a queer cat
Is the meerkat.
It cannot purr or miaow.
And how odd-ish
That no dogfish
Knows how to bow-wow-wow.
The ladybird
Is seldom heard
To tweet, and never sings.
And that wombat's
Too round and fat
To be a mouse with wings.
There are no ants
Like eleph ants,
None even near their size.
And guinea pigs
Aren't mini pigs
And don't inhabit sties
While the mongoose
Is a wrong goose.
You'll seldom see one fly.
And bushbabies
Are hushed babies
That hardly ever cry.

Nick Toczek

Mad Gardener's Song

He thought he saw an Elephant,
 That practised on a fife:
He looked again, and found it was
 A letter from his wife.
'At length I realize,' he said,
 'The bitterness of Life!'

He thought he saw a Buffalo
 Upon the chimney-piece:
He looked again, and found it was
 His Sister's Husband's Niece.
'Unless you leave this house,' he said,
 'I'll send for the Police!'

He thought he saw a Rattlesnake
 That questioned him in Greek:
He looked again, and found it was
 The Middle of Next Week.
'The one thing I regret,' he said,
 'Is that it cannot speak!'

He thought he saw a Banker's Clerk
    Descending from the bus:
He looked again, and found it was
    A Hippopotamus:
'If this should stay to dine,' he said,
    'There won't be much for us!'

He thought he saw a Kangaroo
    That worked a coffee-mill:
He looked again, and found it was
    A Vegetable-Pill.
'Were I to swallow this,' he said,
    'I should be very ill!'

He thought he saw a Coach-and-Four
    That stood beside his bed:
He looked again, and found it was
    A Bear without a Head.
'Poor thing,' he said, 'poor silly thing!
    'It's waiting to be fed!'

Lewis Carroll

The Blind Men and the Elephant

It was six men of Hindostan,
To learning much inclined,
Who went to see the elephant,
(Though all of them were blind);
That each by observation
Might satisfy his mind.

The first approached the elephant,
And happening to fall
Against his broad and sturdy side,
At once began to bawl,
'Bless me, it seems the elephant
Is very like a wall.'

The second, feeling of his tusk,
Cried, 'Ho! what have we here
So very round and smooth and sharp?
To me 'tis mighty clear
This wonder of an elephant
Is very like a spear.'

The third approached the animal,
And happening to take
The squirming trunk within his hands,
Then boldly up and spake;
'I see,' quoth he, 'the elephant
Is very like a snake.'

The fourth stretched out his eager hand
And felt about the knee,
'What most this mighty beast is like
Is mighty plain,' quoth he;
''Tis clear enough the elephant
Is very like a tree.'

The fifth who chanced to touch the ear
Said, 'Even the blindest man
Can tell what this resembles most;
Deny the fact who can,
This marvel of an elephant
Is very like a fan.'

The sixth no sooner had begun
About the beast to grope
Than, seizing on the swinging tail
That fell within his scope,
'I see,' cried he, 'the elephant
Is very like a rope.'

And so these men of Hindostan
Disputed loud and long,
Each of his own opinion
Exceeding stiff and strong,
Though each was partly in the right,
And all were in the wrong!

John Godfrey Saxe

Mr McGuire

Old Mr McGuire, blind as a bat,
had a rabbit, a weasel, a dog and a cat.
He stroked them all as he sat by the fire,
some days they felt smooth,
and some days like wire.
With a bark, a hiss, a squeak and miaow
they demanded attention
and all got it somehow.
Old Mr McGuire, he loved them all –
'To me you're one creature
you're all from the same sack.
God brought you here
and he'll take you back.
You may think you're all different
but, heavens above –
you are all of you loved
with one single love.'

Brian Patten

Wonderful Worms

Anna Worm is acrobatic,
Bertie Worm is brave,
Charlie Worm is cheerful,
a daring worm is Dave.

Elspeth Worm is elegant,
Freddie Worm has fangs,
Gertie Worm is simply great,
Harvey Worm just hangs.

Ivy Worm's inspiring,
Jasmine Worm, she jives,
Katy Worm is kindly,
Lucy Worm saves lives.

Mary Worm's magnificent,
Nasreen Worm is neat,
Oliver Worm is odd at times,
a popular worm is Pete.

Quentin Worm is quiet and quick,
Richard Worm is wriggly,
Sanjit Worm's surprising,
Tamsin Worm is tickly.

Ulrica Worm is upside down,
Vikram Worm is vexed,
William Worm is witty and wise,
a secretive worm is X.

Yolanda Worm likes yellow sand,
Zoe Worm has zest.
Ask any worm, 'Are you wonderful?'
and all worms answer, 'YES!'

Celia Warren

Song of Mr Toad

The world has held great Heroes,
　　As history-books have showed;
But never a name to go down to fame
　　Compared with that of Toad!

The clever men at Oxford
　　Know all that there is to be knowed.
But they none of them know one half as much
　　As intelligent Mr Toad!

The animals sat in the Ark and cried,
　　Their tears in torrents flowed.
Who was it said, 'There's land ahead'?
　　Encouraging Mr Toad!

The Army all saluted
　　As they marched along the road,
Was it the King? Or Kitchener?
　　No. It was Mr Toad!

The Queen and her Ladies-in-waiting
    Sat in the window and sewed.
She cried, 'Look! who's that *handsome* man?'
    They answered, 'Mr Toad.'

Kenneth Grahame

The Frog

What a wonderful bird the frog are –
When he stand, he sit almost;
When he hop, he fly almost.
He ain't got no sense hardly;
He ain't got no tail hardly either.
When he sit, he sit on what he ain't got almost.

Anon.

The Brushbaby

The Brushbaby
lives under the stairs
on a diet of dust
and old dog hairs

In darkness, dreading
the daily chores
of scrubbing steps
and kitchen floors

Doomed to an endless
Life of grime
My poor little wooden
Porcupine.

Roger McGough

The Porcupie

I should not try, if I were you,
To eat the porcupie;
Although the crust is brown and crisp
And packed with meat, you'll die.
Those little spikes will pierce your throat,
Those quills will make you ill,
And you will find no antidote,
No medicine or pill.
So let the little porcupie
Go quietly to its lair
And satisfy your appetite
With apple, plum or pear;
So porcupies may occupy
A world made safe for porcupies
Here and everywhere.

Vernon Scannell

Little Trotty Wagtail

Little trotty wagtail, he went in the rain,
And tittering, tottering sideways he near got
    straight again.
He stooped to get a worm, and look'd up to catch
    a fly,
And then he flew away, ere his feathers they were
    dry.

Little trotty wagtail, he waddled in the mud,
And left his little footmarks, trample where he would.
He waddled in the water-pudge, and waggle went
    his tail,
And he chirrupt up his wings to dry upon the
    garden rail.

Little trotty wagtail, you nimble all about,
And in the dimpling water-pudge you waddle in
    and out;
Your home is nigh at hand, and in the warm pigsty,
So, little Master Wagtail, I'll bid you a goodbye.

John Clare

The Cuckoo

The cuckoo, O the cuckoo,
A pretty bird is she
Who singeth as she flies
From tree to tree to tree.

In her beak a wild mint leaf
To keep her sweet voice clear
And the more that she singeth
We know summer draweth near.

Anon.

The Eagle

He clasps the crag with crooked hands:
Close to the sun in lonely lands,
Ringed with the azure world, he stands.

The wrinkled sea beneath him crawls;
He watches from his mountain walls,
And like a thunderbolt he falls.

Alfred, Lord Tennyson

Be Like the Bird

Be like the bird, who
Resting in his flight
On a twig too slight
Feels it bend beneath him,
Yet sings
Knowing he has wings.

Victor Hugo

The Bird's Nest

I know a place, in the ivy on a tree,
Where a bird's nest is, and the eggs are three,
And the bird is brown, and the eggs are blue,
And the twigs are old, but the moss is new,
And I go quite near, though I think I should have
    heard
The sound of me watching, if I had been a bird.

John Drinkwater

The Hen

The hen it is a noble beast
But a cow is more forlorner
Standing lonely in a field
Wi' one leg at each corner.

Anon.

Four Ducks on a Pond

Four ducks on a pond,
A grass-bank beyond,
A blue sky of spring,
White clouds on the wing;
What a little thing
To remember for years –
To remember with tears.

William Allingham

The Prayer of the Little Ducks

Dear God,
give us a flood of water.
Let it rain tomorrow and always.
Give us plenty of little slugs
and other luscious things to eat.
Protect all folk who quack
and everyone who knows how to swim.
Amen.

Carmen Bernos de Gasztold
translated by Rumer Godden

I Saw a Ship a-Sailing

I saw a ship a-sailing
A-sailing on the sea
And oh but it was laden
With lovely things for me

There were chocolates in the cabin
And ice cream in the hold
The sails were made of candyfloss
And the masts were all of gold

The four-and-twenty sailors,
That stood between the decks
Were four-and-twenty white mice
With ribbons round their necks

The captain was a duck
With a parrot on his back
And when the mice were naughty
The captain said Quack! Quack!

Anon.

Penelope's Hats

Aunt Penelope really doesn't like hats
    she wears cushions up there instead
She says they are warm in the winter
    and soft if she falls on her head.

But cushions and pillows are no good
    to wear on your head in the rain.
Like sponges they fill up with water
    and for hours they drip as they drain.

So Penelope wears, when it's raining,
    a duck (one leg tied to each ear).
It's waterproof, and uncomplaining,
    she says, except when given to fear.

In thunderstorms, when all the lightning
    flashes and crashes all night,
the poor duck will quack in a frenzy
    and flap wings with all of its might.

And sometimes, if Penny is running,
   the flapping's enough to take flight,
and the duck and the aunt will go soaring
   up into the sky out of sight.

A. F. Harrold

The Look

The heron's the look of the river.
The moon's the look of the night.
The sky's the look of forever.
Snow is the look of white.

The bees are the look of the honey.
The wasp is the look of pain.
The clown is the look of funny.
Puddles are the look of rain.

The whale is the look of the ocean.
The grave is the look of the dead.
The wheel is the look of motion.
Blood is the look of red.

The rose is the look of the garden.
The girl is the look of the school.
The snake is the look of the Gorgon.
Ice is the look of cool.

The clouds are the look of the weather.
The hand is the look of the glove.
The bird is the look of the feather.
You are the look of love.

Carol Ann Duffy

Snakestanger

An old dialect rhyme about the blood-sucking dragonfly said
to sting only boys who were naughty.

Snakestanger, snakestanger, flee aal about the
   brooks,
Sting ahl the bad bwoys a-slingin their vish hooks;

But let the good bwoys katch aal the vish they can,
And carri 'em away wome to vry 'em in a pan;

Bread and butter they shall yeat at zupper wi' their
   vish
While aal the littul bad bwoys shall only lick the
   dish.

Anon.

The Bee's Knees

Great hairy knees bees have as they squat
in the flowers then push off with a spring,
all six knees pumping and shoving.
With so much power they're soon airborne,
   resilient, muscular, adrift.

The bee's knees.

Brilliant.

George Szirtes

Bees

Bees
have small furry pelts
hard to keep from getting sticky.

Their languages
are dance and telepathy.

Inside each bee
is delicate machinery
a noisy watch mechanism.

Some kamikaze freely for the Empress.
Others, at the end, look back with pride
on an 8 oz jar in the supermarket.

Peter Goldsworthy

Spelling Bees

In the hive at the bottom
Of the garden live 26 bees

I have named each one
After a letter of the alphabet

A swarm is unreadable
But when they land on flowers to refuel

Or settle on the lawn to sunbathe
They spell out words like these:

sprodxk, ytplinew, hucadtr,
zdikql, wlhurbd, xseznm

It's a difficult language
The language of bees.

                                        Roger McGough

Poetry

poetry don't have to be
living in a library
there's poetry that you can see
in the life of everybody,
a lick of paint's the kind of thing I mean
a lick of paint's a lovely piece of writing
the tongue of the paintbrush
giving something drab
a dab new sheen
a lick of paint's exciting.

there are folk who like to see
Latin in their poetry
and plenty of obscurity
me for instance
(only joking)
how I like to listen to the lingo
in bingo
legs eleven
clickety-click
a lick of paint
no – sorry that ain't one

poetry – language on a spree
I want to be
a leaf on the poetree
poetry is good for me
I think I'll have some for my tea

John Hegley

The Uncertainty of the Poet

I am a poet.
I am very fond of bananas.

I am bananas.
I am very fond of a poet.

I am a poet of bananas.
I am very fond,

A fond poet of 'I am, I am' –
Very bananas,

Fond of 'Am I bananas,
Am I?' – a very poet.

Bananas of a poet!
Am I fond? Am I very?

Poet bananas! I am.
I am fond of a 'very'.

I am of very fond bananas.
Am I a poet?

Wendy Cope

OIC

I'm in a 10der mood today
& feel poetic, 2;
4 fun I'll just – off a line
& send it off 2 U.

I'm sorry you've been 6 o long;
Don't B disconsol8;
But bear your ills with 42de,
& they won't seem so gr8.

Anon.

The WOW!

If History is the *When?*
And Science the *How?*
If Philosophy is the *Why?*
Then Poetry is the **Wow!**

Roger McGough

Travel

The railroad track is miles away,
    And the day is loud with voices speaking,
Yet there isn't a train goes by all day
    But I hear its whistle shrieking.

All night there isn't a train goes by,
    Though the night is still for sleep and
    dreaming
But I see its cinders red on the sky
    And hear its engine steaming.

My heart is warm with the friends I make,
    And better friends I'll not be knowing,
Yet there isn't a train I wouldn't take,
    No matter where it's going.

Edna St Vincent Millay

From a Railway Carriage

Faster than fairies, faster than witches,
Bridges and houses, hedges and ditches,
And charging along like troops in a battle,
All through the meadows the horses and cattle:
All of the sights of the hill and the plain
Fly as thick as driving rain;
And ever again, in the wink of an eye,
Painted stations whistle by.

Here is a child who clambers and scrambles,
All by himself and gathering brambles;
Here is a tramp who stands and gazes;
And there is the green for stringing the daisies!
Here is a cart run away in the road,
Lumping along with man and load;
And here is a mill, and there is a river;
Each a glimpse and gone for ever!

Robert Louis Stevenson

The Six Strings

The guitar
makes dreams weep.
The sobbing of lost souls
escapes from
its open mouth.
And like the tarantula
it weaves a huge star
to catch the sighs
that float
from its black
wooden box.

Federico García Lorca

Tarantella

Do you remember an Inn,
Miranda?
Do you remember an Inn?
And the tedding and the spreading
Of the straw for a bedding,
And the fleas that tease in the High Pyrenees,
And the wine that tasted of the tar,
And the cheers and the jeers of the young
    muleteers
(Under the vine of the dark verandah)?
Do you remember an Inn, Miranda,
Do you remember an Inn?
And the cheers and the jeers of the young
    muleteers
Who hadn't got a penny,
And who weren't paying any,
And the hammer at the doors and the Din?

And the Hip! Hop! Hap!
Of the clap
Of the hands to the twirl and the swirl
Of the girl gone chancing,
Glancing,
Dancing,
Backing and advancing,
Snapping of the clapper to the spin
Out and in –
And the Ting, Tong, Tang of the Guitar!
Do you remember an Inn,
Miranda?
Do you remember an Inn?

Never more,
Miranda,
Never more.
Only the high peaks hoar:
And Aragon a torrent at the door.
No sound
In the walls of the Halls where falls
The tread
Of the feet of the dead to the ground,
No sound:
But the boom
Of the far Waterfall like Doom.

Hilaire Belloc

This Poem . . .

This poem is dangerous: it should not be left
Within the reach of children, or even of adults
Who might swallow it whole, with possibly
Undesirable side-effects. If you come across
An unattended, unidentified poem
In a public place, do not attempt to tackle it
Yourself. Send it (preferably, in a sealed container)
To the nearest centre of learning, where it will be
   rendered
Harmless, by experts. Even the simplest poem
May destroy your immunity to human emotions.
All poems must carry a Government warning.
   Words
Can seriously affect your heart.

Elma Mitchell

The Strawberry-Yogurt Smell of Words

Once we made a telephone
– string, stretched between two yogurt pots.
'Hello? Hello?'
Communication!
You spoke. I heard.

It's a solitary game now,
the thumb-dance of text, beep of fax,
but I still recall the buzz of string,
the strawberry-yogurt
smell of words.

Mandy Coe

A Dictionary of Snow

The Eskimos
have lots of words
for snow

There's fine snow
thick snow
blizzard snow
snow for building igloos . . .

Here's my list of words
for snow

splatty is for making snowballs
swoooosh is for sledging through
skolOSH is for kicking with your wellies
smooolly lies on the pavement waiting for
    footprints
shlumpish goes up and down over grassy fields
    until birds make patterns in it
squalOOM is to skid along in the playground
    before the caretaker throws sand on it

skulptush packs together squeaking in your hands
   as you build a snowman
I still need new words for the snow you wipe
off the tops of walls
as you run along the street
and for the sort that cakes
and melts on mittens
after a whole playtime

Rita Ray

To Lalla, Reading my Verses Topsy-Turvy

Darling little Cousin,
    With your thoughtful look
Reading topsy-turvy
    From a printed book

English hieroglyphics,
    More mysterious
To you, than Egyptian
    Ones would be to us; –

Leave off for a minute
    Studying, and say
What is the impression
    That those marks convey?

Only solemn silence,
    And a wondering smile:
But your eyes are lifted
    Unto mine the while.

In their gaze so steady
	I can surely trace
That a happy spirit
	Lighteth up your face.

Tender, happy spirit,
	Innocent and pure;
Teaching more than science,
	And than learning more.

How should I give answer
	To that asking look?
Darling little Cousin
	Go back to your book.

Read on: if you knew it,
	You have cause to boast:—
You are much the wisest,
	Though I know the most.

Christina Rossetti

The Dictionary Bird

Through my house in sunny weather
Flies the Dictionary Bird
Clear to see on every feather
Is some outlandish word.

'Hugger Mugger' 'gimcrack' 'guava'
'Waggish' 'mizzle' 'swashing rain'
Bird – fly back into my kitchen,
Let me read those words again.

Margaret Mahy

Driven to Distraction

I picked up a bus in the High Street
then put it down on the park,
I drove my mum to Distraction –
that's the next town on from Dunkirk.

I stood, like a lemon, in a downpour
and someone gave me a squeeze,
I gave the cold shoulder to Matthew,
in minutes it started to freeze.

I got into hot water for fibbing,
the water didn't tell me a thing,
I threw bread at a tree for a lark
but instead it decided to sing.

I turned up my nose at the dinner,
it stayed like that for a week,
I tried not to be a wet blanket,
but my shoe laces started to leak.

Chrissie Gittins

Pencil World

Your pencil's amazing,
a magical stick.
It might make anything.
Take your pick:

a house on a hill
or a ship at sea,
a bus full of people,
a picture of me,

a fruit or a flower,
a battered old ball,
elephants, igloos,
anything at all.

Everything's in it,
tightly curled,
waiting to wake
from pencil world.

Tony Mitton

Bookish

They prop open windows; let butterflies in,
and stop doors from slamming in sudden, cold wind.

They help with my balance and make me walk tall.
They'll increase my height on a chair if I'm small.

I use them to lean on when tables aren't free
and they're handy for dinners while watching TV.

They can flatten a rose to a paper keepsake
or hide the right answers in tests that I take.

Pile them like pillows at the end of the bed.
Conversation and pictures held inside my head.

Rachel Rooney

Just a Book?

It's a letter in a bottle
bobbing blindly in the sea,
it's a verdant leaf in summer
hanging halfway up a tree,
it's a pebble sleeping softly
in a gently flowing brook
but it's never, no it's never,
no it's *never* just a book.

It's the topping on your pizza
as it sits upon your plate,
it's the fish that you've been after
as you hook it with your bait,
it's a cupboard of ingredients
all waiting for the cook
but it's never, no it's never,
no it's *never* just a book.

It's a soldier in a battle
as he launches a grenade,
it's a hunter in a forest
as she sharpens up her blade,
it's a playmate, it's a bully,
it's a policeman, it's a crook
but it's never, no it's never,
no it's *never* just a book.

It's a parcel of ideas,
it's a package full of tools,
it's a field full of freedom,
it's a folder full of rules,
it's a fancy flight of fantasy
so come and have a look –
see it's never, no it's never,
no it's *never* just a book!

Joshua Seigal

Today I Read a Bus Stop

Today I read a bus stop
and then I read a van,
a poster and three carrier bags,
some shop signs and a man
who had a crazy T-shirt on.

I'd already read the cereal box,
a mug, and the jam label
and the headlines of the paper
that was lying on the table.

I read some writing in the sky,
I even read the road,

a tree, a sign stuck in the grass,
some number plates that whistled past,

a bag of crisps, a birthday card
(it had my name on it so that was easy).

I was reading a text message
when I should have read the door
so then I pushed instead of pulled
and dropped my mobile on the floor.

Then I started on this poem
and went out for another look

because

reading is amazing
and all the world's a book.

Kathy Henderson

Wise One

Wise one, wise one
how long is a piece of string?

Twice as long as half its length.

Wise one, wise one
how do you kill a snake?

Put its tail in its mouth
and it'll eat itself up.

Wise one, wise one
What's at the end of cat's tail?

A cat.

Wise one, wise one
How can I get a chick out of a boiled egg?

Feed it to the chicken
so it can lay it again.

Wise one, wise one
Why do bricklayers put mortar on bricks?

To keep the bricks together
and to keep the bricks apart.

Wise one, wise one
My parrot talks too much.

Give it a good book to read.

Michael Rosen

Apostrophe

How nice to be
an apostrophe
floating
above an *s*

hovering
like a paper kite
in between the *it's*

eavesdropping
tiptoeing
high above the *that's*

an inky comet
spiralling
the highest tossed
of hats.

Roger McGough

Comma

How, great,
to, be, a, comma,
and, Separate,
one, word, fromma,

nother.

Brian Bilston

Comparisons

As wet as a fish – as dry as a bone;
As live as a bird – as dead as a stone;
As plump as a partridge – as poor as a rat;
As strong as a horse – as weak as a cat;
As hard as a flint – as soft as a mole;
As white as a lily – as black as a coal;
As plain as a staff – as rough as a bear;
As light as a drum – as free as the air;
As heavy as lead – as light as a feather;
As steady as time – uncertain as weather;
As hot as an oven – as cold as a frog;
As gay as a lark – as sick as a dog;
As savage as tigers – as mild as a dove;
As stiff as a poker – as limp as a glove;
As blind as a bat – as deaf as a post;
As cool as a cucumber – as warm as toast;
As flat as a flounder – as round as a ball;
As blunt as a hammer – as sharp as an awl;
As brittle as glass – as tough as gristle;
As neat as a pin – as clean as a whistle;
As red as a rose – as square as a box;
As bold as a thief – as sly as a fox.

Anon.

Back Room Boy

I wrote the poem that Tommy read
In assembly today
I volunteered to be the one
Who puts the paints away

I am the playtime monitor
I take Miss Moss her tea
If someone's needed for a job
Then that someone is me

I passed the ball to Sarah
And Sarah scored the goal
I rehearsed the play with Tina
Prepared her for the role

I like to work behind the scenes
Not in the spotlight's glare
But I thought I'd write this poem
To remind you I am there

Roger Stevens

A Song about Myself

There was a naughty boy,
   And a naughty boy was he,
He ran away to Scotland
   The people for to see —
      There he found
      That the ground
      Was as hard,
      That a yard
      Was as long,
      That a song
      Was as merry,
      That a cherry
      Was as red —
      That lead
      Was as weighty,
      That fourscore
      Was as eighty,
      That a door
      Was as wooden
      As in England —
So he stood in his shoes
      And he wonder'd

He wonder'd,
He stood in his
Shoes and he wonder'd.

John Keats

A Boy's Song

Where the pools are bright and deep,
Where the grey trout lies asleep,
Up the river and o'er the lea,
That's the way for Billy and me.

Where the blackbird sings the latest,
Where the hawthorn blooms the sweetest,
Where the nestlings chirp and flee,
That's the way for Billy and me.

Where the mowers mow the cleanest,
Where the hay lies thick and greenest;
There to trace the homeward bee,
That's the way for Billy and me.

Where the hazel bank is steepest,
Where the shadow falls the deepest,
Where the clustering nuts fall free,
That's the way for Billy and me.

Why the boys should drive away
Little sweet maidens from the play,
Or love to banter and fight so well,
That's the thing I never could tell.

But this I know, I love to play,
Through the meadow, among the hay;
Up the water and o'er the lea,
That's the way for Billy and me.

James Hogg

The Magic Pebble

My favourite thing is a pebble
That I found on a beach in Wales
It looks like any other
But its magic never fails

It does my homework for me
Makes difficult sums seem clear
School dinners taste delicious
It makes teachers disappear

It turns water into lemonade
A bully into a frog
When I'm in need of company
It becomes a friendly dog

One, two, three and *Whoosh!*
You're in a foreign land
Space travel is so easy
Simply hold it in your hand

Close your eyes and make a wish
And wish your wish comes true
For the magic in this pebble
Has been waiting here for you.

Roger McGough

The Magic of the Brain

Such a sight I saw:
An eight-sided kite surging up into a cloud
Its eight tails streaming out as if they were one.
It lifted my heart as starlight lifts the head
Such a sight I saw.

And such a sound I heard.
One bird through dim winter light as the day was
    closing
Poured out a song suddenly from an empty tree.
It cleared my head as water refreshes the skin
Such a sound I heard.

Such a smell I smelled:
A mixture of roses and coffee, of green leaf and
    warmth.
It took me to gardens and summer and cities
    abroad,
Memories of meetings as if my past friends were
    here
Such a smell I smelled.

Such soft fur I felt:
It wrapped me around, soothing my winter-
    cracked skin,
Not gritty or stringy or sweaty but silkily warm
As my animal slept on my lap, and we both
    breathed content
Such soft fur I felt.

Such food I tasted:
Smooth-on-tongue soup, and juicy crackling of
    meat,
Greens like fresh fields, sweet-on-your-palate peas,
Jellies and puddings with fragrance of fruit they
    are made from
Such good food I tasted.

Such a world comes in:
Far world of the sky to breathe in through your
    nose
Near world you feel underfoot as you walk on the
    land.
Through your eyes and your ears and your mouth
    and your brilliant brain –
Such a world comes in.

Jenny Joseph

I Saw a Peacock

I saw a peacock with a fiery tail
I saw a blazing comet drop down hail
I saw a cloud wrapped with ivy round
I saw an oak creep along the ground
I saw an ant swallow up a whale
I saw the sea brim full of ale
I saw a Venice glass five fathoms deep
I saw a well full of men's tears that weep
I saw red eyes all of flaming fire
I saw a house bigger than the moon and higher
I saw the sun at twelve o clock at night
I saw the man who saw this wondrous sight.

Anon.

The Grammarian Saw a Peacock

I saw a peacock
A blazing comet with a fiery tail
A cloud drop down hail
An oak wrapped with ivy round
An ant creep along the ground
The sea swallow up a whale
A Venice glass brim full of ale
A well five fathoms deep
Red eyes of men's tears that weep
A house all of flaming fire
The sun bigger than the moon and higher
At twelve o clock at night
I saw the man who saw this wondrous sight.

RMCG

What Is Pink?

What is pink? a rose is pink
By a fountain's brink.
What is red? a poppy's red
In its barley bed.
What is blue? the sky is blue
Where the clouds float thro'.
What is white? a swan is white
Sailing in the light.
What is yellow? pears are yellow,
Rich and ripe and mellow.
What is green? the grass is green,
With small flowers between.
What is violet? clouds are violet
In the summer twilight.
What is orange? why, an orange,
Just an orange!

Christina Rossetti

First Morning

I was there on that first morning of creation
when heaven and earth occupied one space
and no one had heard of the human race.

I was there on that first morning of creation
when a river rushed from the belly of an egg
and a mountain rose from a golden yolk.

I was there on that first morning of creation
when the waters parted like magic cloth
and the birds shook feathers at the first joke.

John Agard

A Feather from an Angel

Anton's box of treasures held
a silver key and a glassy stone,
a figurine made of polished bone
and a feather from an angel.

The figurine was from Borneo,
the stone from France or Italy,
the silver key was a mystery
but the feather came from an angel.

We might have believed him if he'd said
the feather fell from a bleached white crow
but he always replied, 'It's an angel's, I know,
a feather from an angel.'

We might have believed him if he'd said,
'An albatross let the feather fall.'
But he had no doubt, no doubt at all,
his feather came from an angel.

'I thought I'd dreamt him one night,' he'd say,
'but in the morning I knew he'd been there;
he left a feather on my bedside chair,
a feather from an angel.'

And it seems that all my life I've looked
for that sort of belief that nothing could shift,
something simple yet precious as Anton's gift,
a feather from an angel.

Brian Moses

The Treasures

Who will bring me the hush of a feather?
'I,' screeched the Barn Owl. 'Whatever the
   weather.'

Who will bring me the shadows that flow?
'I,' snarled the Tiger. 'Wherever I go.'

Who will bring me the colours that shine?
'I,' shrieked the Peacock. 'Because they are mine.'

Who will bring me the crash of the wave?
'I,' sang the Dolphin. 'Because I am brave.'

Who will bring me the secrets of night?
'I,' called the Bat. 'By the moon's silver light.'

Who will bring me the scent of the flower?
'I,' hummed the Bee. 'By the sun's golden power.'

Who will bring me the waterfall's gleam?
'I,' sighed the Minnow. 'By river and stream.'

Who will bring me the strength of the small?
'I,' cried the Spider. 'When webs line your wall.'

Who will bring me the shiver of snow?
'I,' howled the Wolf Cub. 'When icicles grow.'

And who will bring me a nest, furry warm?
'I,' squeaked the Rat, 'When we hide from the
    storm . . .
But who will care for the treasures we give?'

'I,' said the Child.
'For as long as I live.'

Clare Bevan

A Memory

Honey holds a memory of bees
Salt holds a memory of seas

Snow holds a memory of cold
Rock holds a memory of gold

Lily holds a memory of white
Moon holds a memory of bright

Bear holds a memory of sleep
River holds a memory of deep

Cloud holds a memory of sky
Mountain holds a memory of high

Wood holds a memory of tree
The world holds a memory of ME

Louise Greig

A Drop in the Ocean

Sloshing around
in life's restless sea,
there's a drop in the ocean –
and that drop is me.

Riding the waves,
or washed up on the shore,
I'm a minuscule drop
amongst zillions more.

I'm a drop in the ocean
of life's restless sea –
but there'd be no ocean
without drops like me!

Jane Clarke

Voices of Water

The water in the rain says
                    Tick Tick Tack
The water in the sleet says
                    Slush
The water in the ice says
                    Crick Crick Crack
The water in the snow says
                    Hush

The water in the sink says
                    Slosh Slosh
The water in the tap says
                    Drip
The water in the bath says
                    Wash Wash
The water in the cup says
                    Sip

The water in the pool says
                    Splish Splash
The water in the stream says
                    Trill
The water in the sea says
                    Crish Crash
The water in the pond . . .
                    stays still.

The water in the soil says
                    Sow, Sow
The water in the cloud says
                    Give
The water in the plant says
                    Grow, Grow
The water in the world says
                    Live

                    Tony Mitton

Roots

It's a quiet job
being a root.
No one hugs you,
climbs you
or praises your
intricate ways.

Roots work
in the dark.
And it's hard work
tunnelling,
travelling,
finding nutrition.

But when
the storms come
it's our fingers
which cling.
When the drought comes
it's our lips
that drink.

Without us
the ground would crumble.
Without us
life would fall.

Everyone
needs roots.

Steve Turner

Bulb

Smooth fingers touch my papery skin,
place me in soil
in a shallow hole, cover me.

Loam and grains soothe,
and trickling water comforts.

I rest; seem dead, but only sleep.
I wait.

And all at once, a tingle urges
slender threads to slip from me,
roots to feed me,
roots to anchor me.

And then my head surges
and a shoot, green as a frog,
forces up through earth,
reaches the light.

I shall burst with brilliance,
a blazing trumpet of daffodil
blaring at the sun.

When my yellow fades
to crisp parchment, I shall stay
in my secret cavern, know worm and beetle,
feel my strength return
for next year's flowering.

Alison Chisholm

from Home Thoughts from Abroad

Oh, to be in England
Now that April's there,
And whoever wakes in England
Sees, some morning, unaware,
That the lowest boughs and the brushwood sheaf
Round the elm-tree bole are in tiny leaf,
While the chaffinch sings on the orchard bough,
In England – now!

Robert Browning

A Slash of Blue

A slash of Blue —
A sweep of Gray —
Some scarlet patches on the way,
Compose an Evening Sky —
A little purple — slipped between
Some Ruby Trousers hurried on —
A Wave of Gold —
A Bank of Day —
This just makes out the Morning Sky.

Emily Dickinson

Loveliest of Trees

Loveliest of trees, the cherry now
Is hung with bloom along the bough,
And stands about the woodland ride
Wearing white for Eastertide.

Now, of my threescore years and ten,
Twenty will not come again,
And take from seventy springs a score,
It only leaves me fifty more.

And since to look at things in bloom
Fifty springs are little room,
About the woodlands I will go
To see the cherry hung with snow.

A. E. Housman

The Sensation of Well-Being

The sensation of well-being,
  Which my heart from yours receives,
Is like the deep content a tree
  Finds in its fresh green leaves.

Farrukhi

In the Tree's Defence

Trees are good at what they do,
at being oak or beech or yew.

They shake their leaves to make a breeze
and pop out blossom for the bees.

In crook of branch they'll hold a nest
which, birds concur, is for the best.

On rainy days they shield the feller
who's forgot his umbrella.

In summer they provide the shade
for picnickers out in the glade.

Inside their sturdy hearts of wood
trees are simply doing good.

A. F. Harrold

from *Blueberries*

'You ought to have seen what I saw on my way
To the village, through Patterson's pasture today:
Blueberries as big as the end of your thumb,
Real sky-blue, and heavy, and ready to drum
In the cavernous pail of the first one to come!
And all ripe together, not some of them green
And some of them ripe! You ought to have seen! . . .

'You ought to have seen how it looked in the rain,
The fruit mixed with water in layers of leaves,
Like two kinds of jewels, a vision for thieves.'

Robert Frost

Beetroot

The beetroot is a bossy veg,
inside it's deep maroon,

it comes into your kitchen
and paints the entire room.

The juice gets on your fingers,
the juice gets on the walls,

when you rinse your fingers –
a red Niagara Falls!

The beet leaps on the oven
and tells you what to do –

'Bake me, boil me, grate me,
slice me with a knife,

whizz me into tasty soup
but don't go through your life

without my redness on your tongue;
enjoy my velvet texture –

then sing this Beetroot Song!'

Chrissie Gittins

Fish and Chips

Fish and chips today for tea,
A fish for Gran, a fish for me.
I buy them at the corner place,
From smiling Meg of rosy face.

Meg sees the small boys lick their lips
At battered fish and golden chips.
Her apron's white, her hands are red;
She sees the hungry thousands fed.

For sixpence more there're peas as well,
Mushy peas with gorgeous smell;
And butter beans on Friday night,
Pale, steaming beans for your delight.

The counter's white, the walls are pink,
The shelves hold lemonade to drink.
The fat is hissing in the pan,
And soon I hurry home to Gran.

The chips look good, they taste the same,
They've won our Meg some local fame.
Fish and chips today for tea,
A fish for Gran, a fish for me.

A. Elliott-Cannon

The Potatoes My Dad Cooks

Let me now praise the potatoes my Dad cooks
    for truly they are epic;

for they come from the oven smelling so sweet,
    their smell delights my nostrils

and when they sit steaming in their dish,
    their crispy coatings delight my eyes

and when I take one up and bite it,
    the coating breaks with a crunch

and when I chew that mouthful,
    the mouthful delights my tongue

and then it delights my throat,
    and then, oh then it warms my insides,

for truly the potatoes of my Dad are epic.
    The potatoes of his enemies will fail.

Joanne Limburg

The Storm

See lightning is flashing,
The forest is crashing,
The rain will come dashing,
   A flood will be rising anon;

The heavens are scowling,
The thunder is growling,
The loud winds are howling,
   The storm has come suddenly on!

But now the sky clears,
The bright sun appears,
Now nobody fears,
   But soon every cloud will be gone.

Sara Coleridge

The Wind in a Frolic

The wind one morning sprung up from sleep,
Saying, 'Now for a frolic! now for a leap!
Now for a mad-cap, galloping chase!
I'll make a commotion in every place!'
So it swept with a bustle right through a great town,
Creaking the signs, and scattering down
Shutters; and whisking, with merciless squalls,
Old women's bonnets and gingerbread stalls.
There never was heard a much lustier shout,
As the apples and oranges trundled about;
And the urchins, that stand with their thievish
    eyes
For ever on watch, ran off each with a prize.

Then away to the field it went blustering and
    humming,
And the cattle all wondered whatever was coming;
It plucked by their tails the grave, matronly cows,
And tossed the colts' manes all about their brows,
Till, offended at such a familiar salute,
They all turned their backs, and stood sullenly mute.
So on it went, capering and playing its pranks:

Whistling with reeds on the broad river's banks;
Puffing the birds as they sat on the spray,
Or the traveller grave on the king's highway.
It was not too nice to hustle the bags
Of the beggar, and flutter his dirty rags:
'Twas so bold, that it feared not to play its joke
With the doctor's wig, or the gentleman's cloak.

Through the forest it roared, and cried gaily, 'Now,
You sturdy old oaks, I'll make you bow!'
And it made them bow without more ado,
Or it cracked their great branches through and
    through.
Then it rushed like a monster on cottage and farm,
Striking their dwellers with sudden alarm;
And they ran out like bees in a midsummer swarm.
There were dames with their 'kerchiefs tied over
    their caps,
To see if their poultry were free from mishaps;
The turkeys they gobbled, the geese screamed aloud,
And the hens crept to roost in a terrified crowd;
There was rearing of ladders, and logs laying on
Where the thatch from the roof threatened soon to
    be gone.

But the wind had passed on, and had met in a lane,
With a schoolboy, who panted and struggled in
　　vain;
For it tossed him, and twirled him, then passed,
　　and he stood,
With his hat in a pool, and his shoe in the mud.

There was a poor man, hoary and old,
Cutting the heath on the open wold –
The strokes of his bill were faint and few,
Ere this frolicsome wind upon him blew;
But behind him, before him, about him it came,
And the breath seemed gone from his feeble frame;
So he sat him down with a muttering tone,
Saying, 'Plague on the wind! was the like ever
　　known?
But nowadays every wind that blows
Tells one how weak an old man grows!'

But away went the wind in its holiday glee;
And now it was far on the billowy sea,
And the lordly ships felt its staggering blow,
And the little boats darted to and fro,
But lo! it was night, and it sank to rest,
On the sea-bird's rock, in the gleaming west,
Laughing to think, in its fearful fun,
How little of mischief it had done.

William Howitt

The Windmill

Behold! a giant am I!
    Aloft here in my tower,
    With my granite jaws I devour
The maize, the wheat, and the rye,
    And grind them into flour.

I look down over the farms;
    In the fields of grain I see
    The harvest that is to be,
And I fling to the air my arms,
    For I know it is all for me.

I hear the sound of flails
    Far off, from the threshing-floors
    In barns, with their open doors,
And the wind, the wind in my sails,
    Louder and louder roars.

I stand here in my place,
    With my foot on the rock below,
    And whichever way it may blow
I meet it face to face,
    As a brave man meets his foe.

And while we wrestle and strive,
    My master, the miller, stands
    And feeds me with his hands;
For he knows who makes him thrive,
    Who makes him lord of lands.

On Sundays I take my rest;
    Church-going bells begin
    Their low, melodious din;
I cross my arms on my breast,
    And all is peace within.

H. W. Longfellow

Daybreak

On the tidal mud, just before sunset,
dozens of starfishes
were creeping. It was
as though the mud were a sky
and enormous, imperfect stars
moved across it as slowly
as the actual stars cross heaven.
All at once they stopped,
and as if they had simply
increased their receptivity
to gravity they sank down
into the mud; they faded down
into it and lay still; and by the time
pink of sunset broke across them
they were as invisible
as the true stars at daybreak.

Galway Kinnell

The Moon and a Cloud

Sometimes I watch the moon at night,
    No matter be she near or far;
Up high, or in a leafy tree
    Caught laughing like a bigger star.

Tonight the west is full of clouds;
    The east is full of stars that fly
Into the cloud's dark foliage,
    And the moon will follow by and by.

I see a dark brown shabby cloud –
    The moon has gone behind its back;
I looked to see her turn it white –
    She turned it to a lovely black.

A lovely cloud, a jet-black cloud;
    It shines with such a glorious light,
That I am glad with all my heart
    She turned it black instead of white.

W. H. Davies

The Star

Twinkle, twinkle, little star,
How I wonder what you are!
Up above the world so high,
Like a diamond in the sky.

When the blazing sun is gone,
When he nothing shines upon,
Then you show your little light,
Twinkle, twinkle, all the night.

Then the traveller in the dark,
Thanks you for your tiny spark,
He could not see which way to go,
If you did not twinkle so.

In the dark blue sky you keep,
And often through my curtains peep,
For you never shut your eye,
Till the sun is in the sky.

As your bright and tiny spark
Lights the traveller in the dark—
Though I know not what you are,
Twinkle, twinkle, little star.

Jane Taylor

Star

Twinkle, twinkle, little star
Scientists tell us what you are.
Hydrogen . . . and helium?
Oxygen and nitrogen . . .
Twinkle, twinkle, little star
Is that really what you are?

Twinkle, twinkle, little spark
Bravely twinkling in the dark
We come out to gaze at you,
When we worry what to do.
We find up there a ray of light.
A hope, a comfort in the night
Twinkle, twinkle little star!
Is hope and comfort what you are?

Twinkle, twinkle, I have a clue!
They say we're made of stardust too.
Made to shine, made to gleam
To imagine and to dream
Twinkle, twinkle, little star
– a friend to us is what you are.

Twinkle, twinkle, little child,
In the garden running wild
Full of laughter, free and light
I hope your future will be bright,
Twinkle, twinkle, you'll go far
Shine on bravely – you're the star.

Michaela Morgan

Stars

Stars

are to reach for,
beautiful freckles of hope,
speckles on velvet,
to steer ships,
to comfort those trapped in the darkness of their
    making,
to lead the wayward when the compass falters,
to remind us that the day is almost breaking,
dawn is just out – taking time to warm the other
    side of the world.

Stars are for wishes.

Stars are
tiny lights of hope,
fireflies in the night,
golden specks to gaze at,
tin tacks on a dark cloth,
studs glittering,
sequins on a first party dress.

Stars are
our brightest and best,
shards of hope to keep us going,
marking the place,
marking the seasons, giving us purpose
because somewhere out there

there are other star gazers
gazing back.

Pie Corbett

Comet

(To be read as quickly as possible, in as few breaths as you can manage.)

I'm a spinning, winning, tripping, zipping, super-
   sonic ice queen:
see my moon zoom, clock my rocket, watch me
   splutter tricksy space-steam.

I'm the dust bomb, I'm the freeze sneeze, I'm the
   top galactic jockey
made (they think) of gas and ice and mystery bits
   of something rocky.

Oh I sting a sherbet orbit, running rings round star
   or planet;
should I shoot too near the sun, my tail hots up:
   ouch – OUCH – please fan it!

And I'm told I hold the answer to the galaxy's top
   question:
that my middle's made of history (no surprise I've
   indigestion)

but for now I sprint and skid and whisk and bolt
   and belt and bomb it;
I'm that hell-for-leather, lunging, plunging, helter-
   skelter COMET.

Kate Wakeling

Winter Morning

Winter is the king of showmen,
Turning tree stumps into snow men
And houses into birthday cakes
And spreading sugar over lakes.
Smooth and clean and frosty white,
The world looks good enough to bite.
That's the season to be young,
Catching snow flakes on your tongue.

Snow is snowy when it's snowing,
I'm sorry it's slushy when it's going.

Ogden Nash

February Twilight

I stood beside a hill
   Smooth with new-laid snow,
A single star looked out
   From the cold evening glow.

There was no other creature
   That saw what I could see –
I stood and watched the evening star
   As long as it watched me.

Sara Teasdale

Night

The sun descending in the west,
   The evening star does shine;
The birds are silent in their nest,
   And I must seek for mine.
The moon, like a flower,
In heaven's high bower,
With silent delight
Sits and smiles on the night.

William Blake

One Bright September Morning

One bright September morning in
   the middle of July,
The sun lay thick upon the ground,
   the snow shone in the sky.
The flowers were singing gaily,
   the birds were full of bloom;
I went upstairs to the cellar
   to clean a downstairs room.
I saw ten thousand miles away
   a house just out of sight,
It stood alone between two more
   and it was black-washed white.

Anon.

Pleasant Sounds

The rustling of leaves under the feet in woods and
    under hedges;
The crumping of cat-ice and snow down wood-
    rides, narrow lanes, and every street causeway;
Rustling through a wood or rather rushing, while
    the wind halloos in the oak-top like thunder;
The rustle of birds' wings startled from their nests
    or flying unseen into the bushes;
The whizzing of larger birds overhead in a wood,
    such as crows, puddocks, buzzards;
The trample of robins and woodlarks on the brown
    leaves, and the patter of squirrels on the green
    moss;
The fall of an acorn on the ground, the pattering
    of nuts on the hazel branches as they fall from
    ripeness;
The flirt of the groundlark's wing from the
    stubbles – how sweet such pictures on dewy
    mornings, when the dew flashes from its brown
    feathers!

John Clare

Where Go the Boats?

Dark brown is the river,
    Golden is the sand.
It flows along for ever,
    With trees on either hand.

Green leaves a-floating,
    Castles of the foam,
Boats of mine a-boating –
    Where will all come home?

On goes the river
    And out past the mill,
Away down the valley,
    Away down the hill.

Away down the river,
    A hundred miles or more,
Other little children
    Shall bring my boats ashore.

Robert Louis Stevenson

from The Cataract of Lodore

From its sources which well
In the Tarn on the fell;
From its fountains
In the mountains,
Its rills and its gills;
Through moss and through brake,
It runs and it creeps
For a while, till it sleeps
In its own little lake.
And thence at departing,
Awakening and starting,
It runs through the reeds
And away it proceeds,
Through meadow and glade,
In sun and in shade,
And through the wood-shelter,
Among crags in its flurry,
Helter-skelter,
Hurry-scurry.
Here it comes sparkling,
And there it lies darkling;
Now smoking and frothing

Its tumult and wrath in,
Till in this rapid race
On which it is bent,
It reaches the place
Of its steep descent.

The Cataract strong
Then plunges along,
Striking and raging
As if a war waging
Its caverns and rocks among:
Rising and leaping,
Sinking and creeping,
Swelling and sweeping,
Showering and springing,
Flying and flinging,
Writhing and ringing,
Eddying and whisking,
Spouting and frisking,
Turning and twisting,
Around and around
With endless rebound!
Smiting and fighting,
A sight to delight in;
Confounding, astounding,
Dizzying and deafening the ear with its sound.

Collecting, projecting,
Receding and speeding,
And shocking and rocking,
And darting and parting,
And threading and spreading,
And whizzing and hissing,
And dripping and skipping,
And hitting and splitting,
And shining and twining,
And rattling and battling,
And shaking and quaking,
And pouring and roaring,
And waving and raving,
And tossing and crossing,
And flowing and going,
And running and stunning,
And foaming and roaming,
And dinning and spinning,
And dropping and hopping,
And working and jerking,
And guggling and struggling,
And heaving and cleaving,
And moaning and groaning;

And glittering and frittering,
And gathering and feathering,
And whitening and brightening,
And quivering and shivering,
And hurrying and scurrying,
And thundering and floundering;

Dividing and gliding and sliding,
And falling and brawling and sprawling,
And driving and riving and striving,
And sprinkling and twinkling and wrinkling,
And sounding and bounding and rounding,
And bubbling and troubling and doubling,
And grumbling and rumbling and tumbling,
And clattering and battering and shattering;

Retreating and beating and meeting and sheeting,
Delaying and straying and playing and spraying,
Advancing and prancing and glancing and
    dancing,
Recoiling, turmoiling and toiling and boiling,
And gleaming and streaming and steaming and
    beaming,
And rushing and flushing and brushing and
    gushing,

And flapping and rapping and clapping and
    slapping,
And curling and whirling and purling and twirling,
And thumping and plumping and bumping and
    jumping,
And dashing and flashing and splashing and
    clashing;
And so never ending, but always descending,
Sounds and motions for ever and ever are
    blending,
All at once and all o'er, with a mighty uproar,
And this way the Water comes down at Lodore.

Robert Southey

Empty Places

I like empty places.

The woods, the stream, the fields.

It's knowing I've no need
to make connections with anyone
about anything.

It's knowing I don't have to speak,
and that no one can contact me.

And the places themselves
are secure in their silence.
The landscape keeps tight-lipped,
it has no wish to reveal
its secrets.

(Although, just occasionally
I detect the whisperings of leaves,
the gossip of greenery.)

There are times, of course,
when my fingers feel the pulse of the city,
when its heartbeat connects with mine.
There are times too
when I need to be vocal,
when I need to crack the surface of silence.

But then it's back to those empty places,
that desire to be somewhere where no one else is,
to feel, to touch, to surf the breeze.

I like empty places,
the woods, the stream, the fields,
those kinds of places
that I can fill
with my dreams.

Brian Moses

Out in the Desert

Out in the desert lies the Sphinx
It never eats and it never drinx
Its body's quite solid without any chinx
And when the sky's all purple and pinx
(As if it was painted with coloured inx)
And the sun it ever so swiftly sinx
Behind the hills in a couple of twinx
You may hear (if you're lucky) a bell that clinx
And also tolls and also tinx
And they say at the very same sound the Sphinx
It sometimes smiles and it sometimes winx
But nobody knows just what it thinx.

Charles Causley

Contentment

I'm glad the sky is painted blue:
And the earth is painted green;
And such a lot of nice fresh air
All sandwiched in between.

E. C. Bentley

Sun is Laughing

This morning she got up
On the happy side of the bed,
Pulled back
The grey sky-curtains
And poked her head
Through the blue window
Of heaven,
Her yellow laughter
Spilling over,
Falling broad across the grass,
Brightening the washing line,
Giving more shine
To the back of a ladybug
And buttering up all the world.

Then, without any warning,
As if she was suddenly bored,
Or just got sulky
Because she could hear no one
Giving praise
To her shining ways,
Sun slammed the sky-window closed

Plunging the whole world
Into greyness once more.

O Sun, moody one,
How can we live
Without the holiday of your face?

Grace Nichols

Changing Places

The day is disappearing,
she's off to meet the night
where she will share with darkness
the present that is light,

like sunrise, sparkling oceans,
the middle of July,
the oak tree and the blue jay,
the hopscotch butterfly.

The day is disappearing
as light begins to fade,
the night-time's tinsel treasures
are ready to parade:

the helicopter fireflies
and bats in cloak-like flight,
the comets, stars and planets,
the grotto of the night.

So let us praise the noon-shine
and celebrate the night.
The diamanté darkness
and the dancing light.

Stewart Henderson

Smile

Smile, go on, smile!
Anyone would think, to look at you,
that your cat was on the barbecue
or your best friend had died.
Go on, curve your mouth.
Take a look at that beggar,
or that one-legged bus conductor.
Where's *your* cross?
Smile, slap your thigh.
Hiccup, make a horse noise,
lollop through the house,
fizz up your coffee.
Take down your guitar
from its air-shelf and play
imaginary reggae
out through the open door.
And smile, remember, smile,
give those teeth some sun,
grin at everyone,
do it now, go on, SMILE!

Matthew Sweeney

Acknowledgements

The compiler and publisher would like to thank the following for permission to use copyright material:

Ahlberg, Allan: 'Picking Teams' from *Please Mrs Butler* by Allan Ahlberg (Puffin, 2013). Copyright © Allan Ahlberg, 1984; **Agard, John:** 'First Morning' copyright © 1990 by John Agard, reprinted by permission of John Agard c/o Caroline Sheldon Literary Agency Ltd; **Alborough, Jez:** 'A Smile' copyright © Jez Alborough. Reprinted by permission of the author; **Berry, James:** 'Isn't My Name Magical' from *A Story I Am In: Selected Poems* (Bloodaxe Books, 2011), copyright © James Berry. Reprinted by permission of Bloodaxe Books; **Bevan, Clare:** 'The Treasures' copyright © Clare Bevan, first published in *Poems to Perform* by Julia Donaldson (Macmillan Children's Books, 2013). Reprinted by permission of the author; **Bilston, Brian:** 'Hope on a Rope' and 'Comma', copyright © Brian Bilston. Reprinted by permission of the author; **Bloom, Valerie:** 'Keeping Wicket' © 2000 Valerie Bloom, from *Give the Ball to the Poet*, reprinted by permission of the author; **Chisholm, Alison:** 'Bulb' from *A Time to Speak and a Time to Listen* (Schoefiled and Sons, 2013), copyright © Alison Chisholm. Reprinted by permission of the author ;**Clarke, Jane:** 'A Drop in the Ocean', copyright © Jane Clarke, first published in *Don't Get Your Knickers in a Twist* by Paul Cookson (Macmillan Children's Books, 2002). Reprinted by permission of the author; **Clerihew Bentley, E.:** 'Contentment' from *The Complete Clerihews of Clerihew Bentley*, copyright © E. Clerihew Bentley 1963. Reprinted by permission of Curtis Brown Group Ltd, London on behalf of the Estate of E Clerihew Bentley; **Coe, Mandy:** 'The Strawberry-Yogurt Smell of Words' copyright © Mandy Coe. First published in *If You Could See Laughter* (Salt Publishing, 2010). Reprinted by permission of the author; **Coelho, Joseph:** 'Siblings' from *Werewolf Club Rules* by Joseph Coelho, published by Frances Lincoln Ltd, copyright © 2014, reprinted by permission of Frances Lincoln Ltd, an imprint of The Quarto Group; **Cookson, Paul:** May You Always ©Paul Cookson, reprinted by permission of the author; **Cope, Wendy:** 'The Uncertainty of the Poet' copyright © Wendy Cope, reprinted by permission of Faber and Faber; **Corbett, Pie:** 'Stars', copyright © Pie Corbett. Reprinted by permission of the author; **Cowling, Sue:** 'The Laughter Forecast', copyright © Sue Cowling, reprinted by permission of the author; **de la Mare, Walter:** 'The Cupboard', copyright © The Literary Trustees of Walter de la Mare, reprinted by permission granted by their representatives The Society of Authors; **Dean, Jan:** 'Three Good Things' first published in *A Poem for Every Night of the Year* (Macmillan Children's Books, 2017) copyright © Jan Dean, used by permission of the author; **Duffy, Carol Ann:** 'The Look' from *The Hat* by Carol Anne Duffy (Faber and Faber 2007), copyright © Carol Ann Duffy, reproduced by permission of the author c/o Rogers, Coleridge & White Ltd; **Farjeon, Eleanor:** 'Cats' from *Blackbird has Spoken* by Eleanor Farjeon (Macmillan Children's Books, 1999), copyright © Eleanor Farjeon, reprinted by permission of David Higham Associates; **Frost, Robert:** from 'Blueberries' from *Poetry of Robert Frost* by Robert Frost (published by Jonathan Cape), reprinted by permission of The Random House Group Limited. Canadian permissions provided by Henry Holt and Company from The *Poetry of Robert Frost* edited by Edward Connery Lathem, copyright © 1969 Robert Frost; **Gittins, Chrissie:** 'Driven to Distraction', first published in *Now You See Me, Now You...* (Rabbit Hole Publications, 2002) and 'Beetroot', first published in *Adder, Bluebell, Lobster* (Otter-Barry Books, 2016), copyright © Chrissie Gittins, reprinted by permission of the author; **Goldsworthy, Peter:** 'Bees' copyright © Peter Goldsworthy, used by arrangement with the licensor, Peter Goldsworth, c/o Curtis Brown (Aust) Pty Ltd; **Greig, Louise:** 'A Memory' copyright © Louise Greig, reprinted by permission of the author; **Harrold, A. F.:** 'Penelope's Hats' and 'In the Tree's Defence' copyright © A. F. Harrold, reprinted by permission of the author. **Hegley, John:** 'Poetry' copyright © John Hegley1991, reprinted by permission of United Agents; **Henderson, Kathy:** 'Today I Read a Bus Stop' from *The Dragon with a Big Nose* by Kathy Henderson (published by Frances Lincoln Ltd), copyright © 2013, reprinted by permission of Frances Lincoln Ltd, an imprint of The Quarto Group; **Henderson, Stewart:** 'Paintings that Move' and 'Changing Places' from the collection *All Things Weird and Wonderful* by Stewart Henderson (published by Lion Children's Books) copyright © Stewart Henderson 2003; **Henri, Adrian:** 'Best Friends' by Adrian Henri (published by Methuen, 1986), copyright © Adrian